Choose Your Bully

A novel by

Lori Jamison

HIP-JR.

HIP Junior
Copyright © 2005 by High Interest Publishing

Library and Archives Canada Cataloguing in Publication

Jamison, Lori, 1955-
    Choose your bully / Lori Jamison.

(HIP jr)
ISBN 1-897039-15-8

I. Title. II. Series.

PS8619.A67C48 2005   jC813'.6   C2005-905372-0

General editor: Paul Kropp
Text design and typesetting: Laura Brady
Illustrations drawn by: Matt Melanson
Cover design: Robert Corrigan

3 4 5 6 7   13 12 11 10 09

Printed and bound in Canada

High Interest Publishing is an imprint of the
Chestnut Publishing Group

Sam and Richard have a great idea to deal with their school bully — hire a bodyguard. But when their bodyguard starts to bully them, they have to get even smarter.

CHAPTER 1

We've Got a Problem

We all have problems. Some kids think they're too tall. Or they're too short. Or their feet are way too big. Or they forget their homework too much. My friend Richard has a funny problem. He's too rich.

Richard's problem begins with his name. He's been called Richie Rich for years. Kids say, "Oh, look, there's Richie Rich." Then all the other kids laugh. My friend would say, "My name is Richard," and they'd all laugh again.

Of course, Richard does not have any money himself. His parents are rich. His dad works at the bank — my mom says he *owns* the bank — and his mom is a lawyer. But Richard doesn't get much spending money. His parents tell him that he has to learn "the value of money." Most of us had that figured out in grade three.

And money can be a problem. When people *think* you have money, they bug you about it. Guys are always coming up to Richard and begging. "Can you let me have a couple of bucks till next week?" they say. "I'm just a little short of cash for lunch. You'll help me out, won't you?"

When Richard says he doesn't have money, no one believes him. They think — rich parents, rich kid. Then they think he's cheap. Or they try to take the money he does have.

Of course, Richard is not the only one with problems. I've got a few, too. To start with, I hate my name. My name is Ling, but kids have called me Ding-a-Ling since grade one. You can imagine the jokes. *What's the ring tone on Ling's cell phone?*

Ding-a-ling! Ding-a-ling! My parents can't afford a cell phone, but that's a problem I can't fix.

Richard and I have one problem in common. Our problem is a bully — and his name is Chuck. Chuck has been taking our money and lunches for months.

"I wish you were a guy," Richard said to me. "Then you could just beat him up."

"Right," I replied. "You're a guy. Why don't *you* beat him up."

"Because I'm too short," Richard admitted. "Because I'm a wimp."

Both those things were true. Richard has always been small for his age. He was a wimp back in daycare. He was a wimp in kindergarten. Richard was scared to climb the climbers, scared to slide the slide. He was afraid of mice, snakes, frogs and all sorts of cool things. Of course all the kids made fun of him.

I am *not* a wimp. I'm pretty gutsy, even if I am a girl. I once hit Chuck on the head and made him cry. I was about five years old, so Chuck must have been six. We were at the playground. Chuck was grabbing my sand pail. I said stop. He didn't stop, so I whacked him on the head. He cried and my mom got mad at me.

I think that was the last time anyone beat up on Chuck. Now that Chuck is 13, he's bigger than all of us. He's got lots of pimples and the start of a moustache. He's also a full head taller than me. If I wanted to whack him on the head now, I'd need to get up on a chair.

As I said, Chuck is a bully. There are *sometimes* bullies and *all-the-time* bullies. A sometimes bully is a kid who might pick on you once a month. A sometimes bully gets mad at you and says he'll beat you up. But a sometimes bully only talks tough. When it comes to a fight, the sometimes bully won't show up.

But Chuck is an all-the-time bully. He is a bully when he wakes up in the morning. He's a bully on the way to school. He's a bully at lunch, on the way home, and after school. He just likes picking on other kids.

The kid Chuck picks on the most is Richard.

"You have to stop being a victim," I said to Richard. We were walking to school early in the morning. It was October

"So how do I do that?" he asked.

"Stand up for yourself."

"Easy for you to say," he said. He made a strange face. Richard is pretty funny-looking most of the time. When Richard makes a face, he's *very* funny looking.

"If you stand up for yourself, the bully will pick on some other kid," I said. I had read that in a book once.

"Yeah?"

"Don't just give in like a wuss. Tell Chuck no and just keep saying no."

Richard shook his head, then he looked up ahead. There was Chuck. He was waiting for us. Chuck had been waiting for us almost every day since school began.

Richard's face turned white.

Chuck just smiled at us. "Richie Rich, you are right on time," Chuck said. "I need some lunch money."

CHAPTER 2

The World According to Chuck

The three of us just stared at each other. I could feel my muscles get really tight. I wanted to whack Chuck on the head with a sand pail again, like I did seven years ago.

"I don't have any money today," Richard said.

I stared at Richard, hard. I tried to give him courage. I tried to send him my thoughts — *don't give in. Don't back down.*

"Yeah, like I really believe that." Chuck laughed at him. "You've got more money than any kid in

this town. Now pay up, or get beat up."

I could see Richard start to cave. *Be strong,* I thought to him. But Richard got this scared look on his face, like he was going to cry. Richard doesn't cry any more. But he does *look* like a victim.

So I had to stand up for him. "Richard said no," I said for my friend. "No means no."

"Shut up . . . Ding-a-Ling," Chuck snapped back. "This is between Richie Rich and me. Unless you want to pay the toll for him."

"There is no such thing as a toll sidewalk," I said. This is true. There are toll highways and toll house cookies. But there are no toll sidewalks.

"And I said shut up," Chuck said. He turned back to Richard and held out his hand. "Two bucks today," he demanded.

"I . . . I don't have two bucks," Richard told him.

There was a sneer on Chuck's face. He just stood there, holding out his hand, tapping his foot on the sidewalk.

I tried to send another thought to Richard —

Just say no. But I guess my thought didn't get to him.

"I've only got fifty cents," Richard said. His voice was shaky.

"That'll do, for a start," Chuck told him.

So Richard took off his backpack and began to look for money.

If there had been an adult around, I could have shouted for help. But there was nobody in sight. I didn't know the people who lived nearby. I couldn't see anybody. It was just us . . . and Chuck.

Two or three days each week, it was us and Chuck. Two of three days each week, Richard would pay the "toll." By now, Richard must have handed over ten bucks or more. Even worse, there was no end in sight. Chuck could wait for us for the rest of our lives. Chuck could demand his "toll" until we all got out of high school.

Somehow this had to stop.

"Richard, don't give him anything!" I shouted.

Richard looked up. Chuck turned his big ugly head toward me.

"Shut up, Ling."

"I mean it, Richard," I said. "You don't have to pay this jerk. This is robbery. This is theft. I'm going to call the cops."

"With what?" Chuck shot back, laughing.

He knew I didn't have a cell phone. Richard *had* a cell phone — but then Chuck broke it. So now we had no way to call anyone.

Richard found two quarters in his backpack and gave them to Chuck. My friend had an awful look on his face. He looked like he'd been beaten up — and Chuck hadn't even touched him. I thought, for a second, that Richard might cry. When we were little, Richard used to cry a lot, but he's tougher now. He just cries on the inside.

"I'll take the lunch, too," Chuck said. He reached into the backpack and grabbed it.

"Hey," Richard began, "you said . . ."

That's when I lost it. I had seen this happen, again and again, and I was sick of it. I couldn't watch my friend get bullied like this. And I didn't feel like sharing my lunch with Richard one more time.

So I took off my backpack. Then I grabbed it by the two shoulder straps. And I whacked Chuck on his back and his neck. Then I pulled back and whacked him again — hard.

For a second, I think he was too stunned to do much. When I pulled back to hit him a third time, he turned and got his hand up. As my backpack came down on him, he reached up and pushed it away.

I lost hold of the straps and my backpack fell to the ground.

Chuck just laughed at me, then kicked my backpack so it slid across the grass. I had good stuff in there, and he just kicked it. If I was mad before, I was even madder now!

So I came at him with my fists. I got a good hit into his shoulder with my right fist, but then he grabbed both my hands. We were face to face. I was as mad as I've ever been. He was just laughing.

"So what now, Chuck? You going to hit a . . . girl?" I figured if he could use the "girl" word as an insult, I'd throw it back at him.

"Keep it up and I will."

"What a man!" I said, mocking him. "What a jerk!"

Chuck got as mad as I was. Then he gave me an answer to my question. No, Chuck would not hit a girl. But he'd sure give a girl one big push.

Chuck's push sent me flying backwards. I tried not to fall, but my feet must have slipped on the wet grass. Anyhow, I went backwards and landed on my butt.

"You jerk," I spat right at him.

Chuck laughed right at me. Then he picked up Richard's lunch and walked off to school. No, it was worse than that. He sauntered off to school. There's a big word that means "walked proudly."

How dare he steal a lunch, push me down, and then *saunter* to school.

How dare he!

CHAPTER 3

We Need a Plan

Richard helped me to my feet and got my backpack from the lawn. I brushed away some leaves, but the rear of my jeans was wet. Talk about embarrassing!

"You were a big help," I said. When I get mad, I can get mad at anybody close by. With Chuck gone, Richard was my only target.

"I thought you were going to beat him up," Richard said. "You almost did."

"Yeah, right," I told him. "The guy weighs 50

pounds more than me. And he's way taller. And he's strong as an ox. But you thought I could beat him up," I said, giving Richard a look. "Let's get real."

"You have a point," Richard said.

"Aaagh!" I cried. Of all the things to say, *you have a point* must be the dumbest. No wonder kids picked on Richard.

We had to run to get to school on time, so there was no more time to think. Later, when we saw Chuck at recess, he just grinned at us. He was already eating some of Richard's lunch. He seemed to enjoy eating it right in front of us.

"Aaagh!" I said to Richard.

"It must be an aaagh kind of day," he replied.

At noon, we had to share my lunch . . . again. My mom always packs too much food, so it's not as if I went hungry. I think Richard likes my lunches more than his. He sure ate his half of the lunch fast enough.

I tried to get my thoughts together, but I was still too mad. It's hard to think clearly when you're

mad. So I waited until I got home. Then I did a Google search on "bullies." My teacher, Ms Barris, says research is a good thing. She's talking about school, of course. But I figured I could research bullies, too.

I printed out some pages and started a file — my "Chuck" file. Then I did some thinking. I thought about the whole "Chuck" problem until my head hurt. Then I made a list of things we could do.

THE CHUCK PROBLEM! SOLUTIONS

1. Get some help — teacher, parents, etc.
2. Fight back. Beat him up, somehow.
3. Find a way to get Chuck to pick on somebody else.
4. Get somebody to drive us to school.
5. Hire a bodyguard.
6. Get a big dog.

All the websites said we should use solution number one. They said kids shouldn't deal with bullies on their own. But who would help us? My mom worked and Richard's parents both had jobs. They were all at work when Chuck bullied us.

And Chuck never did much at school. He knew that the teachers would see what he did, so he pretended to be nice. Nice! Chuck is about as nice as a pit bull. Besides, Ms Barris couldn't help us much *outside* of school. I mean, she's a teacher, not Superman.

We knew that "fight back" wouldn't work. Neither of us was much good at fighting. Nor could I come up with a way so Chuck would pick on somebody else. How do you get some other kid to be a victim? So that left us with the ride, the bodyguard or the dog.

I showed the list to Richard the next day. He made his choice right away.

"I like number six, the dog."

"All the websites say go with number one."

Richard nodded his head, but didn't change his mind. "I just like dogs. My parents won't let me have one. They think a dog will get the house dirty."

Richard's house is *never* dirty. There are whole rooms that we aren't even allowed into. I think his mom is some kind of clean freak.

"I kind of like dogs, too," I told him.

"A big dog would protect us," Richard said, smiling brightly. Then he stopped and looked right at me. "Why don't you ask your mom?"

"Why is it always me?"

"Because your mom is nice and my parents are kind of ..."

"Busy?"

"Not as nice as your mom," Richard said.

So I went to talk to my mom later that day. I didn't say a thing about Chuck. I just said that I wanted a dog and was old enough to take care of one. My mom said a dog would cost too much. She said it wouldn't be fair to leave a dog at home all day. "How about a cat?" was her idea.

A cat couldn't do much against Chuck.

I gave Richard the bad news. "No to the dog. Maybe to a cat. Have you ever heard of a guard cat?"

"No," Richard sighed.

"Me neither," I told him. "So I think we should try a bodyguard."

"You have somebody in mind?"

"Frank Bosco."

"Ooh," Richard said. "Frank the Tank."

Frank Bosco — "Frank the Tank" — was a kid in grade eight who was as big as a truck. He played football. He lifted weights. But Frank was not a nice guy. He liked to beat up kids of various shapes and sizes. He once tried to beat up Richard, but Richard ran off before Frank could get him.

Frank lived just a block away from us. It would be easy for him to follow us to school. Then if Chuck showed up, Frank could come protect us.

"You think Frank would do it?" Richard asked.

"If we paid him," I said. "I figure five bucks a week should do it. That's only a dollar a day."

"We could split it," Richard suggested.

I just looked at him. "Richard, let's be clear about who has the problem here. There are no bullies bugging me."

"You do have a point," he said. Those were becoming his favourite words. "That would be all my lunch money for the week."

"So? Right now, Chuck is taking all your lunch money. And if this bodyguard thing works, we won't need Frank after a couple of weeks."

"How did you get to be so smart?"

"Before I was born, God gave my mom a choice between beauty and brains. She chose brains," I told him. It was an old joke, but seemed pretty good right then. The trouble was, Richard didn't get it.

"Really?" he asked.

"Aaagh!"

CHAPTER 4

Let's Make a Deal

You might wonder how Richard got to be my friend. After all, he's kind of wimpy and not that smart. Like I said before, his family is rich. Richard lives in a very big house with a swimming pool, a tennis court and seven TV sets. (I counted them one day.)

He's about as different from me as he could be. "You two are like chalk and cheese," my mom says. I never quite got that, but it must mean that we don't have much in common.

But when we were little, Richard's parents got my mother to baby-sit him. They would drop Richard off at our house, and then go to work. So Richard was always around. One summer, my mom got sick. She had to go to the hospital for two weeks. So I got to live at Richard's house for two weeks. Now *that* was cool.

Richard taught me how to swim. He taught me to play tennis. He showed me how to play pool. By the end of the summer, we were like brother and sister. We only live a block apart, so it was easy to go back and forth.

So now Richard is my friend for life. It's too bad, really. I'd like to have a *cool* friend, or a really good girl friend. But I've got Richard. That's just how it ended up.

"So when are you talking to Frank?" Richard asked.

"Why do I have to do the talking?" I sighed.

"Because you're good at it," Richard replied. "Besides, Frank doesn't like me. He tried to beat me up once. Remember?"

"That was years ago," I said. "I bet he doesn't even remember you."

Richard gave me this look. "Please?" he begged.

So at lunch it was my job to talk to Frank the Tank. He always hung out with the grade eight kids. They played football at lunch, with four guys on a side. It was touch football, but they still pushed each other a lot. I think that guys who play football are different from guys like Richard who play tennis. The football guys seem to like the pain. They like falling down, and pushing, and getting hit in the head. Pretty strange, if you ask me.

I got to Frank just before the lunch game began.

"Frank, I've got a deal for you," I said.

He gave me a look as if I had lost my mind. "Who are you?"

"I'm Ling," I said, "but most kids call me Ding-a-Ling. Anyhow, I'm looking for somebody who's big and tough and smart. All the kids say that you're the man."

Pretty good buttering up, I said to myself. It

always pays to tell a stupid kid that he's smart. It's always good to tell a big, tough kid that he's big and tough. That way the guy doesn't have to prove it to you.

"So what's this deal?" he asked. "Make it quick, kid. I got a game starting up in a second."

"My friend and I are having some trouble. This guy Chuck has been giving us a hard time. You know how it is."

"Yeah, I know the kid. He's like a bully, right?"

"Right," I said. "So my friend and I could use a little help. You know, a little protection."

"It'll cost you," Frank said.

"How's five bucks a week?"

He gave me a look. I think he was trying to figure out how much I could pay.

"How about ten?"

"You think I'm made of money?" I shot back. "How about five bucks a week and a bonus of five bucks if you have to get in a fight?"

"A ten-buck bonus if there's blood," he said.

"Okay, ten bucks for bleeding. Do we have a deal?"

"Yeah, but I gotta get to my game. We'll work out the rest after school."

The rest, as they say, was details. We met with Frank after school. He wasn't too happy when he saw Richard. I guess he knew Richard could afford more than five bucks a week. But a deal is a deal. Besides, there was that bonus money for a real fight.

We had to give Frank the first five bucks in advance. I figured that would be part of the deal. I had the cash ready, just in case. When the deal was done, we shook hands and agreed to meet the next morning. Then Richard and I headed for his house.

"You think this is a good idea?" he asked.

Richard is like that. He keeps second-guessing himself.

"The best idea so far," I told him.

"I don't like that ten-buck bonus for bleeding," Richard says. "It seems . . . well, kind of sick. I feel like we've hired some guy in a mob."

"Richard, we did not start this," I reminded him. "Nor was the bonus our idea. Remember, it was Frank who put it in the deal."

31

CHAPTER 5

Protection

The next day, our protection began. Richard and I left for school at 8:15. At 8:30 we met Frank. We asked him to walk about a block behind us. If Chuck came up to us, Frank would run up and deal with him.

"Do I just beat him up?" he asked.

"Only if I say so," I told him. I didn't want to pay a bonus if we didn't have to.

"Just look mean and you'll scare him," Richard said.

"How do I look mean?" Frank asked.

Richard and I both looked at him, but I was the one who spoke. "Just be yourself, Frank. Just be yourself."

Wouldn't you know it — Chuck didn't show up. Here we were, all ready to deal with him, and the guy didn't come. Maybe Chuck slept in, or maybe he picked on some other kid to get lunch money. Funny, we were kind of sad not to see him. How's that for strange?

The next day, the same thing. We wondered if Chuck had heard about our protection. Maybe he got word that Frank was on our side. Or maybe Chuck had turned around and become a good guy. Miracles do happen.

But there was no miracle with Chuck. On Friday, we saw him.

"He's waiting for us," Richard said. His voice had gone up really high.

"Good," I said. "Now we can show him who's in charge."

Richard thought about that and then nodded his head. "You have a point, Ling."

We walked halfway up the block. Chuck walked halfway down the block. Actually, Chuck *strutted* halfway down the block. That's a better word. He looked pretty proud of himself.

Chuck didn't even say hello. He just snapped his fingers, put out his fat hand, and said, "Lunch money."

"Don't you ever say *please*?" I asked. I was trying to stall him. I kept waiting for Frank to come running up.

"Not if I can help it," Chuck replied. "And since you're getting mouthy — I'll take lunch money from Richie Rich, here, and lunch from you."

"Over my dead body," I told him. *Where was Frank*? I kept thinking.

"Lunch isn't worthy dying for," Chuck told me. "But I'll give you another big push if you don't hand it over."

I looked over my shoulder. Frank had been behind us since we left my house. He was so big he

36

was easy to see. But now there was nobody. We were on our own.

"Looking for something?" Chuck asked.

"Uh, not really," I said. "I just thought I heard something."

So Richard paid the "toll," his lunch money. And I paid for talking back, my lunch. Later that day, I was the one who had to share Richard's lunch. And I *hate* carrot sticks.

That's when we ran into Frank.

"Where *were* you?" I began. "Chuck shows up, and you're nowhere."

"I went to play football with my buddy," Frank replied. "It's kind of boring following you guys to school. Nothing ever happens. So when my buddy came up, I said to myself, these guys are okay."

"But we weren't okay."

Frank just smiled. "Sorry about that."

When somebody says "sorry about that," you know they're not very sorry at all. Frank was off throwing a football in our hour of need! What kind of bodyguard was that?

"Okay," I said, even though it wasn't okay. "Next week is a new week. We'll just try it again."

"I need another five bucks," Frank told us.

"But you didn't do anything this week," I whined. "When we needed you, you weren't there."

"Just a minor problem," he said. "If you want protection, you gotta pay. Up front. Ahead of time."

I thought about docking him one day's pay, but decided not to. Frank might just quit and then we'd be back where we started. So we agreed to pay. At least Frank would have to show up to get his money.

On Monday morning, Frank showed up right on time. He got his money, then followed behind us. It was a drippy, rainy day. The walk to school wouldn't be a nice one.

And it wasn't. Chuck come up to us, not far from the school. This time I looked back even before Chuck spoke. I saw Frank hanging back, waiting.

"New week, new toll," Chuck told us.

I heard footsteps coming behind us and knew it would be Frank.

"New week, no money," I replied. "The toll highway is now a freeway, Chuck!"

I don't think that Chuck got my witty line. He certainly did not laugh. Then again, he might have been watching Frank run up towards us.

Frank was out of breath when he reached us. For a football player, he wasn't in very good shape.

"Hey, meatball," Frank began. "Are you bugging my friends?"

"These are your friends?" Chuck replied.

"If I say they're my friends, they're my friends." Then Frank reached out with one hand and pointed his index finger right at Chuck. "You got that?"

Chuck looked like he'd swallowed his own tongue. "Uh, I guess."

"So listen up, zit-face," Frank went on. "I don't want to hear about you bugging my friends. No more money, no more stolen lunches. You got it?"

Frank poked his finger into Chuck's chest. Chuck flinched, like it really hurt. Then he looked back and forth at all three of us. I think he was

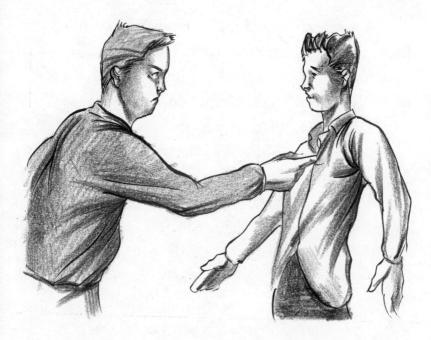

figuring the odds in his head. Maybe he could take on Frank, but it would be one tough fight. Then if I hit him with my backpack, Frank would be all over him. It would be a massacre.

I smiled at my own idea. I even liked the word, massacre.

"Well, okay," Chuck said, backing away. "I got it, Frank. No worries, man."

In just five seconds, Chuck was gone. He went

between two houses, and then must have gone over to High Street. That just left the three of us, making our way to school. We were all feeling pretty good.

"How'd you like the *zit-face* part, eh?" Frank asked. "I came up with that just this morning."

"Very clever, Frank," I told him, even though it wasn't. "You were great."

"Yes, thank you very much," Richard added. Sometimes he's so polite he makes me want to throw up.

"No problem, kid," he said to Richard. "The good news for me is that I finally get that bonus. I want that extra ten bucks tomorrow."

"It's only five dollars," I said. "There wasn't any blood. There wasn't even a fight."

"Yeah, I should charge you even more because I didn't get to fight him," Frank told us. "I kind of missed that part. But I guess ten bucks will be enough."

"Ten bucks for what?" I demanded.

Frank gave me a look as if I were the idiot. "For

CHAPTER 6

Bully, Bully

It feels great when a problem is solved. So long as Chuck bullied us, he was always on my mind. I was angry all the time. Or I was trying to come up with a way to stop him. Or I was dreaming up awful things we could do.

But now, Chuck was gone. Frank had fixed our problem. The whole next week, we kept looking for him. Richard would say, "I think I see him." But it was never Chuck. We went to school each day just like other kids. No tolls to pay. No lost lunches.

It almost felt weird to be normal.

By Friday, we were just having fun again. We would goof around, or tell jokes, or play tag. I even brought a squirt gun on Friday. Ms Barris won't let us bring squirt guns to school. But who says Ms Barris has to know? We never told her about Chuck, and now the problem was fixed.

"You're going to get in trouble," Richard said.

"Only if you tell," I replied. "And if you do, you'll get soaked."

"But she'll take your gun."

"I've got two. It was a two-for-one sale on supersoakers. Try to say that five times fast."

"Two-for-one sale on supersoakers, two-for-one sale of supersoakers, two-for-one sale of soakersupers..."

"I knew you couldn't," I said proudly. "You couldn't get it right three times."

It was that kind of day. We were both feeling kind of silly, kind of happy, kind of carefree. You know how that is. Some days, the sun is shining outside and it's also shining inside. It was really that simple . . . we thought.

Then Frank walked up to us on the way to school.

"Hey guys," he said.

We smiled at him. After all, Frank had fixed our problem. Frank had scared Chuck so badly that we hadn't seen that bully for a whole week.

"Hey, Frank," I said. "Looks like you scared Chuck for good."

"We haven't seen him at all," Richard added.

We were grinning at each other. I think we must have looked pretty strange as a group. Richard and I are both kind of small. On the other hand, Frank is pretty big. We both have to look up at him when we talk.

"Yeah," Frank replied, "I think he's picking on some other kids. I seen him in the park the other day, acting like a goof."

"I *saw* him in the park," I said. I was trying to fix up his grammar.

"Seen, saw . . . what's the diff?"

"No diff," I said. Maybe it's not a good idea to

fix up grammar for a guy who is twice your size.

"Anyhow, I fixed your problem. Right?"

"Right," we agreed.

Frank smiled and we joined in. The Chuck problem was over. Victory! A marching band began playing "We are the Champions" in my head.

"The trouble is," Frank went on, "your problem could come back."

Richard and I just gave him a look. All at once, the marching band in my head stopped playing.

The word "victory" got a question mark. Victory?

"He could come back?" Richard said.

Frank smiled and rubbed his hands together. "Yeah, it's like this. I make this Chuck guy go away, but when I'm not around, he could come back. It's not like Chuck died or went to some other school. He's still around. I didn't even get a chance to beat him up."

"Yes, that was a shame," Richard said.

I turned and gave Richard a look.

"So you need more protection," Frank went on. "You paid for two weeks and got good protection, right? But now you need to keep that protection going. If you don't have me on your side, that guy Chuck will be right back on you."

"You think so?" I asked.

"You can count on it," Frank replied. "Soon as he knows I'm not looking out for you, you guys are toast."

"Toast," Richard sighed.

"So you know how you fix that, don't you?" Frank asked. It was the lead-up to his big idea. "You keep me looking out for you, like, week after week. What's five bucks a week to get rid of somebody like Chuck? I mean, that's like nothing for a kid like you, Richie."

"Right, it's like nothing," Richard groaned.

"Then your problem is solved, like, for good. No problems with Chuck and no problems with me." Frank smiled as he finished. He was like a salesman trying to sell us a used car. He laid out the deal, then waited until we went along with him.

It took a while for all this to sink in. Okay, Frank wanted five dollars a week to keep up protection. But we didn't need protection right now. What if we said no? What would Frank do then? Would he go tell Chuck to come back and bug us . . . or would he start bugging us himself?

"I think Richard and I had better talk about this," I said. I wanted to buy time to think.

"Sure, no problem," Frank replied. "Bring me five bucks every Monday and you'll be fine. I'll be looking out for you all year long. For now, I'll take your super soaker as a small down payment." He grabbed my water gun and walked off.

"Hey, that's mine," I shouted.

Frank turned and grinned at me as he walked into school.

All year long, I said to myself. *This could go on all year long.* We had eight months of school left. That's about 32 weeks. Five dollars a week times 32 weeks equals . . . $160. Ohmygod! That's real money!

"Richard," I whispered so Frank couldn't hear, "we've got *another* problem!"

CHAPTER 7

A Scheme

Problems! People have lots of ways to deal with their problems. My friend Richard, for instance, goes into panic mode.

"We're toast!" he cried. "Now we've got two bullies! This could go on forever! And it was all your idea!"

Richard kept telling me that he voted for solution number six, the dog. He told me that Frank was worse than Chuck. He kept saying it was all my fault.

Some friend.

When I have a problem, I try to get smart. *Think*, I told myself. Things are bad, but there's always a solution. I spent the whole weekend trying to come up with a solution. I went on the Internet. I went to the library and got books. I thought . . . and thought . . . and thought. At last, I had figured it out.

On Sunday night, I walked over to Richard's house for a swim. It was a warm night for the end of October. His pool is heated, and there are these big heaters to keep the deck warm. Boy, it's nice to be rich.

Richard, of course, did not care about the swim. He was worried about Frank.

"Stop worrying," I told him. "I have a scheme."

"A what?"

"A scheme," I said. "You know, like a plan . . . only smarter."

So I told Richard the scheme, and he liked it. We got dried off and then Richard's parents got us ice cream. It was really *good* ice cream, not like the

51

cheap no-name stuff my mom buys. Then we sat out by the pool and wondered if my scheme would work.

On Monday, we still had to pay Frank the five dollars. There was no way out of that. We needed time to get my scheme going. Five bucks bought us time.

On Tuesday, I went to see a girl named Marcie. She was in grade eight and used to live next door to us. I told her that Chuck has been calling Frank a *wuss*. I said that Chuck was saying all kind of things about Frank, behind his back. I said that Chuck was too scared to get in a fight.

On Wednesday, Richard went to see Frank. He told Frank that Chuck was calling him a *wuss*. He said that Chuck had dared Frank to a fight. Richard said that Chuck was telling all the kids the same thing — Frank was too scared to get in a fight.

On Thursday, all the kids were talking. Chuck and Frank were both mad. Chuck called Frank a *wuss*, a chicken, and worse. Frank called Chuck a liar, a coward, a spineless jerk. This was bigger than Richard and me making up stories. It was real.

Thursday was the day Marcie came to see me. "There's going to be a fight," she told me. I asked her when. "On Friday, right after school, in the playground."

"Oh no!" I said. But *excellent* is what I thought.

I walked home with Richard after school. He wasn't happy about this.

"They might find out we started it," he said.

"No way," I replied.

"Somebody could get hurt," he said.

"So?" I told him. "These guys are bullies. They were going to hurt us."

He gave me a look.

"Okay, I'll make sure the fight isn't too bad."

On Friday morning, I went to me Mr. Mac, which is short for Mr. Maciniak. Mr. Mac is our school's gym teacher. He's so tall his head hits the door frame. And he weighs as much as a small whale. He's pretty strong too. Once he lifted a whole car to raise money for the school yearbook.

Anyhow, I told Mr. Mac that there was going to be a fight. He asked me where and when. So I had to tell him . . . kind of.

*   *   *

After school, about 200 kids were waiting at the playground. The word was out — there was going to be a fight. It was Frank against Chuck, a fight to the finish.

Chuck got to the playground first. He was dressed in an old ripped T-shirt and jeans. And he looked mad.

After a while, Frank came to the playground. He came in with a dozen of his buddies. Frank was dressed in his red football jersey and red track pants. His clothes made him look like a fire hydrant.

"Who's going to win?" Richard whispered to me.

"It doesn't matter," I said.

"Why not?"

"We want them to beat each other up," I said. "That's the whole point. Then they won't be bugging us."

"Where's Mr. Mac?"

"He's coming," I said. That was almost true. In fact, I told Mr. Mac that the fight would be at four o'clock. By the time he showed up, the fight should be over.

When Frank came up, the crowd of kids made a space in the middle. That middle space had only two guys — Frank and Chuck.

"You been bad-mouthing me!" Frank shouted.

"You been dissing me!" Chuck replied.

"I ain't gonna let that happen," Frank told him.

"C'mon, fat boy. I'm gonna let you have it!"

It's a good thing Ms Barris wasn't here. She would have taken them both to the office for bad grammar.

As it was, the two bullies began to circle each other. Chuck would come in, and Frank would take a swing. Frank would come in, and Chuck would try to grab him.

On the outside, all the kids were shouting. "Go, go, go!"

At last, the fight started. Frank grabbed Chuck and threw him to the ground. Then he jumped on Chuck and gave him a solid punch. But Chuck pushed Frank off, then kicked him and pushed him. In a second, Frank was on the ground. Chuck was hitting him in the gut. But then Frank gave Chuck a shove with his legs. The shove pushed Frank into the air, and then he fell to the ground.

"This is just like a wrestling match on TV," Richard said.

"Even better," I told him. "This fight is for real."

The fight was going just like I planned. In another few minutes, they would both be beaten up. It didn't much matter who won, they'd both be hurting. That was my whole plan.

Just then, Mr. Mac showed up. He had the principal, Ms Pace, with him. All the kids pushed back to make way for them. While Mr. Mac was big, Ms Pace was *mean*.

Mr. Mac grabbed hold of Chuck. He picked him up and threw Chuck to one side. "Stay there!" he ordered.

Then Mr. Mac lifted up Frank with one hand. He held Frank by his red shirt until Frank stopped wiggling.

By then, Ms Pace had taken hold of Chuck's earlobe. The poor guy was twisting in pain.

"You two come with us," Ms Pace said. "The rest of you," she went on, looking at all of us, "go on home. The show's over."

"Move it!" Mr. Mac shouted at Frank, or maybe at the rest of us.

So we did. All the kids — us too — began to walk away. The last thing I heard was Ms Pace. I'm not sure who she was talking to, but the words were clear. Those were the words I worried about all night.

"I'm going to get to the bottom of this!"

CHAPTER 8

The Best Laid Schemes

On Monday, I was smiling. Both Frank and Chuck had been kicked out of school for three days. They were in big trouble with their parents. And we had made it safely to school with both our lunches and our money.

But then the P.A. went off. "Ms Barris, would you send Richard and Ling to the office?" It was the voice of Ms Pace.

"Of course," our teacher replied. Ms Barris didn't like me much. She would have been glad to send me to the office. But she must have been surprised that Richard was in trouble.

When we got into Ms Pace's office, I could tell this would be bad. Ms Pace had this nasty look on her face. Standing at the window was Mr. Mac, looking like a giant. He wasn't smiling either.

Richard and I just stood there.

"We've been looking into that problem on Friday," Mrs. Pace began. "We've already talked to Frank and Charles . . . and Marcie." She waited for those words to sink in. "Is there anything you two have to say?"

We stood there, scared and awkward. The room was silent. All we could hear was some clock ticking. *Tick . . . tick . . . tick . . . guilty . . . guilty . . . guilty.*

Richard cracked first. "It wasn't my idea," he said.

Thanks a lot, I thought to myself. "We were being bullied," I said.

"It could have gone on forever . . ." Richard

added, and then his voice cracked. It sounded like he was going to cry.

"Oh, I'll tell them," I said.

And then I did. I told them about Chuck and his "toll" and Frank and his "protection." I told them how my friend Richard was always being picked on. I told them that I had lied to Marcie to set up the fight. But I said I had warned Mr. Mac about it.

"You said the fight would start at four o'clock."

I squirmed in my seat. "I was never good at telling time."

"Ling, this is serious," Ms Pace replied.

"I'm sorry," I said. "I made a mistake."

"You know those boys could have been badly hurt," Ms. Pace said.

"Yes," I replied.

"You know it's wrong to spread rumors like that."

"Yes." My feet and hands were kind of twisting. I think my face was red.

That's when Mr. Mac joined in. "Why didn't

you talk to us about the bullying? No one should have to pay a toll to come to school."

Richard answered him. "We didn't think you could do anything. It wasn't on school grounds."

"So instead you had an idea. You decided to have the bullies beat each other up." Ms. Pace shook her head and stared right at me.

I had lost my voice. My words came out like the croak of a frog. "It seemed like a good idea . . . at the time."

"Wrong," said Mr. Mac. "It was a bad idea, any time."

"I'm going to call your parents and tell them what you've done," said Ms Pace. "And then I'm going to put you to work."

More silence. The clock kept on ticking. I wondered if my mom would be mad. I wondered if Richard's parents would ground him. I wondered what the *work* would be.

"I want a two thousand word report," said Ms Pace. "On the best way to handle bullies."

"By getting an adult to help?" I asked.

"Right," replied Ms Pace. "Now you just have 1994 words to go."

I sighed. Maybe Richard was right all along. Maybe we should have gotten a really big dog.

Bats Past Midnight

by SHARON JENNINGS

Sam and Simon wonder about a fancy car that hangs around their school late at night. When they try to find out more, they end up in trouble at school, at home and with the police.

Three Feet Under

by PAUL KROPP

Scott and Rico find a map to long-lost treasure. There's $250,000 buried in Bolton's mine. But when the school bully steals their map and heads for the old mine, the race is on.

The Crash

by PAUL KROPP

A school bus slides off a cliff in a snowstorm. The bus driver is out cold. One of the guys is badly hurt. Can Craig, Rory and Lerch find help in time?

Lori Jamison is a teacher, curriculum consultant and author. She has written several books and articles on exemplary reading and writing instruction, including *Guided Reading Basics* and *The Write Genre*. She was formerly a teacher for the Regina Public Schools in Saskatchewan, then a Language Arts consultant for that board. For the last few years, Lori has prepared teacher's guides for all the HIP novels. She also wrote the novel *Running for Dave* for the HIP Senior series.